Secret PRINCESSES

Movie Magic

ROSIE BANKS

Wishing Star Palace

The Secret Princess Promise

"I promise that I will be kind and brave,

Using my magic to help and save,

Granting wishes and doing my best,

To make people smile and bring happiness."

☆☽ CONTENTS ☾☆

CHAPTER ONE
Fun and Games

"It's our turn now," said Charlotte Williams, rolling the dice. It was Sunday night and her family was playing a board game in their living room. Mum was on a team with Charlotte's twin little brothers but Charlotte and her dad were in the lead!

"Seven!" said her dad, moving their counter along to a green space.

"I'll read the question!" said Harvey, taking a card from the box. "What do you call a group of meerkats?"

Dad and Charlotte looked at each other, their eyes the exact same shade of chocolate brown. Charlotte twiddled one of her brown curls as she tried to think of the answer.

"Any ideas?" Dad asked Charlotte hopefully.

Charlotte shook her head. "I wish Mia was here – she'd know the answer!"

Mia Thompson was Charlotte's best friend. She loved animals and knew lots of cool facts about them. But Mia was far away in England, where Charlotte's family used to live.

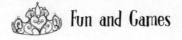

"Time's up!" cried Liam. "What's your answer?"

"We'll just have to guess," said Dad.

"Um," said Charlotte. "Is it a … gaggle?"

"Nope!" crowed Harvey. "A group of meerkats is called a gang, or a mob."

Dad slapped his forehead. "Of course!" he said.

Charlotte giggled and imitated a meerkat on look-out duty. She stuck her head up high and held her hands in front of her like they were paws. In a tough gangster voice she said, "Hey, you! Do ya wanna be in my gang?"

Everyone chuckled.

"You're funny, Charlotte," said Liam.

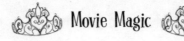

Charlotte grinned. She loved making her family laugh!

Harvey rolled the dice and Liam moved their counter along to an orange space.

"How many innings are there in a baseball game?" asked Charlotte, reading the question on the next card.

"Easy peasy!" gloated Harvey.

"Nine," Liam answered right away.

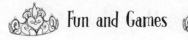

Charlotte's younger brothers had joined a baseball team when they moved to California. They had quickly become experts on the American sport!

"We've got the same number of points as you now!" said Harvey.

"OK," said Mum. "This is the decider. Whoever gets the next question right wins." She slipped a card out of the box. "Who starred in the film *Desert Raiders*?"

"Princess Grace!" Charlotte blurted out, bouncing on her seat in excitement.

Her parents and brothers gave her a strange look and Charlotte suddenly realised what she'd just said. "I mean Grace Devlin!" she corrected herself quickly.

"That's right!" said Mum.

"Woo hoo!" said Dad. "We won!" He gave Charlotte a high five. She smiled weakly in return.

Even though Charlotte was pleased that she and Dad had won the game, she felt terrible. She had almost given away a secret that she'd sworn never to tell!

The movie star Grace Devlin was a princess. But even her biggest fans didn't know that, because Grace wasn't an ordinary princess – she was a Secret Princess who could grant wishes using magic!

If only Mia was here, Charlotte thought. Her best friend was the only person she could talk to about the Secret Princesses.

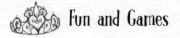

It was because Mia and Charlotte shared
an amazing secret – they were training to
become Secret Princesses too!

"No fair," sulked Liam as they tidied the
board game away. "You and Dad got all the
easy questions."

"Don't be a spoilsport," said Mum, ruffling
Liam's curly hair. "Dad and Charlotte won
fair and square."

"Can we play another game?" asked
Harvey eagerly.

Mum looked at her watch and shook her
head. "It's too late," she said. "You've got
school tomorrow."

"Aw!" grumbled Liam.

"We'll play again soon," promised Mum.

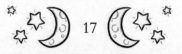

"Go and get ready for bed," said Dad.

Charlotte and her brothers went upstairs and changed into their pyjamas. Then Charlotte went into the bathroom to brush her teeth. Looking in the mirror, Charlotte's eyes lingered on the gold necklace she always wore. There were three white moonstones embedded in the delicate pendant shaped like half of a heart.

Charlotte knew that thousands of miles away in England Mia was wearing a necklace with the other half of the heart. The girls had each earned their three moonstones by granting three wishes. They only needed to grant one more to reach the next stage of their Secret Princess training

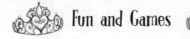
and earn their magic moonstone bracelets!

Charlotte brushed her teeth and bent over the sink to spit out the toothpaste. When she looked up and caught sight of her reflection, Charlotte gasped. Her necklace was glowing!

Holding her pendant, Charlotte whispered, "I wish I could see Mia!"

Dazzling light shone out of the pendant, filling the bathroom with its warm glow. Charlotte squeezed her eyes shut

in anticipation as the light swirled around her, sweeping her away.

A moment later, Charlotte opened her eyes. Three stars twinkled in the night sky, giving out just enough light for Charlotte to spot Wishing Star Palace in the distance. The palace's four white towers gleamed against the black sky.

Glancing down, Charlotte saw that her pyjamas had been magically transformed into a beautiful pink princess dress. The fluffy slippers she'd been wearing at home had been replaced with sparkling magic ruby slippers.

A girl in a gold dress and ruby slippers just like Charlotte's suddenly appeared.

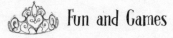

She wore a diamond tiara on her long
blonde hair. It was identical to the one that
rested on Charlotte's brown curls.

"Mia!" cried Charlotte, throwing her arms
around her best friend and spinning her
around. "It's so good to see you!"

Mia laughed as they spun, her blue eyes
shining happily.

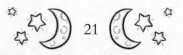

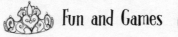
"Hey, Mia," said Charlotte. "Do you know what a group of meerkats is called?"

"A gang," Mia replied instantly.

"I knew you'd know!" Charlotte exclaimed. "My dad and I got that question wrong when we were playing a board game tonight." Charlotte wasn't worried about her family missing her. No time would pass at home while she was at Wishing Star Palace.

"I bet you still won," said Mia.

Charlotte grinned and nodded. "Hey, I wonder if there's a word for a group of Secret Princesses?"

"Hmm," said Mia thoughtfully. "Maybe a 'wish' of princesses? Or a 'glitter'?"

"Or a 'kindness' of princesses," suggested Charlotte.

"Why do you ask?" said Mia.

Charlotte's brown eyes twinkled playfully. She pointed up at the sky. "Because there's a 'glitter' of Secret Princesses heading towards us now!"

CHAPTER TWO
A Glamping Trip

As the princesses got closer, Mia squinted. "What are they riding in?" she asked.

The princesses were waving from the windows of a bright red wagon shaped like a barrel. A magnificent white horse with wings was pulling it through the sky.

"It's an old-fashioned caravan!" exclaimed Charlotte. "A flying one!"

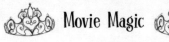

Princess Ella brought
the pretty caravan
down to land neatly on
the grass.

"Hi, everyone," said
Charlotte as the Secret
Princesses opened the
doors and climbed out
of the caravan.

"Hi, Snowdrop," said Mia, patting the
Pegasus's silky mane.

"How are my favourite trainee princesses?"
asked a princess with cool red streaks in her
strawberry-blonde hair. Her necklace had a
pendant shaped like a musical note, because
she was a talented singer.

"Oh, Alice," Charlotte said, hugging her
old friend. "I did something silly at home.
I accidentally said 'Princess' Grace when I
was talking about a movie."

Princess Alice stroked Charlotte's back.
"Don't worry," she said comfortingly.
"There's no harm done. We all know how
hard it is to keep the magic a secret."

Charlotte smiled gratefully at Alice.

Before Alice had become a famous pop star, she'd been Mia and Charlotte's babysitter. Alice had recognised the girls' talent for friendship and invited them to train as Secret Princesses.

A princess with cherry-red hair and a cupcake-shaped pendant nodded. "Everyone slips up sometimes. Once I forgot to take off my tiara at my bakery," Princess Sylvie said. "I had to pretend I was wearing a costume!"

"Speaking of tiaras, has anyone wished on the last tiara star?" asked Mia.

"Not yet," said Princess Luna, fiddling with her moon-shaped pendant anxiously. Back in the real world, she was training

to become an astronaut and she knew all
about the stars.

The Tiara Constellation was a group of
very special stars in the shape of a tiara.
Whenever it appeared in the sky, the Secret
Princesses granted the first wish made on
each of the four stars at the tiara's tips.
These wishes were powerfully magical and
kept Wishing Star Palace safely hidden in
the clouds.

But something terrible had happened
when the constellation had appeared in
the sky. Horrid Princess Poison had used
her bad magic to send a thick green mist
to block out the tiara stars. Princess Poison
had once been a Secret Princess, but she'd

been banished from Wishing Star Palace for using magic to get more power. Now she was threatening the secret of Wishing Star Palace and her curse had stopped Princess Luna's magic from working!

"Don't worry," said Princess Ella, putting her arm around Luna. "Someone will wish on the fourth star soon."

The only way to get Princess Luna's magic back was to grant all four of the tiara star wishes, even though Princess Poison was doing everything she could to spoil them.

"In the meantime, we thought it would be fun to go glamping," said Alice.

"Glamping?" said Charlotte, her forehead wrinkling. "What's that?"

"It's like camping," said Ella.

"But much more glamorous," added Sylvie, grinning.

"But there aren't any tents," said Mia.

"Then we'll just have to magic some up," said Alice. She waved her wand and an exotic purple silk tent appeared.

"Oh, wow!" gasped Charlotte, peering inside the tent. Pretty lanterns cast star-shaped patterns of light on the silk walls. Cushions and leather pouffes were strewn over a luxurious, richly coloured carpet.

"That looks just like a magical flying carpet," said Mia.

"It probably is!" said Charlotte.

"Are you sleeping in here, Sophie?" Mia asked a princess with long brown hair and a pendant shaped like a paintbrush.

"I'm sharing the caravan with Ella," Princess Sophie replied. "Do you want to come and see?"

Charlotte and Mia followed Princess Sophie and peeped inside the little caravan. At one end there were bunk beds covered in cosy patchwork quilts. A dinky little camping stove was at the other end. Enamel mugs and jugs dangled from hooks on the ceiling. Every inch of the caravan's curved ceiling had been decorated with colourful flowers.

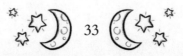

"It's adorable!" exclaimed Charlotte.

"Did you paint the flowers?" asked Mia.

Sophie, who was a talented artist, nodded.

In the middle of the camp, Princess Sylvie used her wand to light a bonfire.

"I miss using my wand," Princess Luna said, sighing. "I wish I could magic up somewhere cool to sleep."

"You can stay with me," said Princess Evie. She pointed her wand at a nearby tree and a huge treehouse appeared in the branches. It looked like a treehouse version of Wishing Star Palace!

Mia and Charlotte followed Evie and Luna up the wooden stairs that spiralled around the tree trunk.

"That's so cool!" gasped Charlotte when they reached the top. The treehouse had hammocks instead of beds!

Mia and Charlotte went out on to the porch. Leaves rustled gently around them and bonfire smoke wafted on the breeze.

"I wish we could get Luna's magic back right now," Mia murmured, gazing up at the sky.

"We will, as soon as someone wishes on the last tiara star," said Charlotte confidently. "We'll grant the wish, then Luna will get her magic back and we'll earn our moonstone bracelets."

"Want to toast marshmallows?" Princess Sylvie called up to them.

Mia and Charlotte thundered down the stairs to join the Secret Princesses around the crackling fire.

Charlotte put a marshmallow on a stick and held it over the bonfire. The flames suddenly turned deep pink!

"Whoa!" she said. "What's going on?" She pulled her marshmallow out of the fire and saw that it had turned pink, too.

"Try it," said Sylvie.

Charlotte blew on her marshmallow to cool it down. Then she took a bite.

It was crisp on the outside and gooey on the inside. "Mmm," said Charlotte. "It tastes like raspberries."

When Mia toasted her marshmallow the flames turned bright yellow.

"Let me guess," said Charlotte as Mia tasted her yellow marshmallow. "Banana?"

"Nope," Mia said, licking her sticky fingers. "Lemon meringue!"

Once they'd all eaten their fill, Princess Evie jumped to her feet. "Who wants to play tag?"

"Isn't it too dark?" asked Charlotte.

Princess Evie tapped the sapphire ring on her finger. Blue light streamed out of the gem. The rings magically glowed when danger was near – but they were also useful torches! She aimed the beam at Charlotte. "Tag!" she cried. "You're it!"

Giggling, Mia and the Secret Princesses ran off to hide.

Charlotte tapped her own sapphire ring. She swept the blue light around, searching for her friends. "Gotcha!" she shouted as the beam caught Princess Sophie hiding behind a tree.

Suddenly, Charlotte noticed a new light. It wasn't coming from a sapphire ring – it was in the sky!

"Time out, everyone!" she hollered. "I think someone's made a wish on the last tiara star!"

The Secret Princesses ran out from their hiding places. They looked up at the four stars shining overhead.

"Can we grant the wish?" Mia asked.

"Yes, please!" said Princess Luna.

Holding hands, Mia and Charlotte clicked the heels of their ruby slippers together three times. "The Astronomy Tower!" they cried.

Their magic slippers carried them to the top of one of Wishing Star Palace's turrets. Charlotte pointed the enormous gold telescope in the middle of the room at the fourth tiara star. Peering through the lens, she saw who had made the wish. It was a girl with dark shoulder-length hair.

"She looks really excited," Charlotte said, stepping aside so that her friend could look through the telescope.

"The message has appeared," Mia said. She read it aloud:

Touch the telescope to see a star.
Call Montana's name and you'll go far.

Holding on to the telescope, Mia and Charlotte shouted, "Montana!"

Charlotte felt wind rush against her face as she and Mia were catapulted through the night sky. The tiara constellation flashed past them, its stars sparkling like diamonds.

"Hang on, Montana," she shouted into space. "We're coming!"

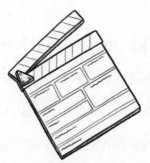

CHAPTER THREE
Elf Yourself

The first thing Charlotte saw when she landed was a huge, hairy troll stomping out of a wood. He had green skin, a hunched back, long nails and teeth like tombstones.

Oh no, Charlotte thought, staring at the troll in alarm. *Something's wrong. The magic has sent us to another world!*

The troll swung a spiky club menacingly.

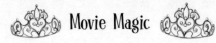

"Surrender, elf!" he growled.

An elf with long, silvery hair and pointy ears aimed his bow and arrow at the troll. "We will never surrender our kingdom," he said defiantly, even though he was much smaller than the enormous troll.

"Mia!" Charlotte gasped. "We've got to try and help him!" Grabbing Mia's hand, she darted forwards.

"Shh!" whispered a woman dressed in black, blocking their way. She was holding a clapperboard that said *Elf Wars* and had a walkie-talkie clipped to her belt.

Charlotte looked around and saw a movie camera, fluffy microphones on long poles and large lights shining on the troll and elf.

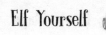

"It's not a different world … it's a film set!" she realised out loud.

The woman holding the clapperboard nodded, then put her finger to her lips and went back to the movie camera.

Mia and Charlotte watched the rest of the scene in silence. The elf fired an arrow at the troll, who howled in rage.

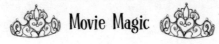

Movie Magic

"Cut!" cried a woman in black-framed glasses sitting behind the movie camera. The back of her canvas chair said *Director*.

The movie set instantly burst into activity as crew members hurriedly moved equipment around. Mia and Charlotte jumped out of the way as someone wheeled wooden crates marked *Danger – Fireworks* past them.

"Can you see Montana anywhere?" asked Charlotte, standing on her tiptoes to look round.

"Maybe we should go over there," suggested Mia, pointing to a sign marked *Base*. They came to a cluster of trailers parked by the edge of the woods. A group of

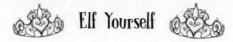

children were sitting in the sunshine outside the trailers. Some were reading books, chatting or playing cards. The girl from the telescope had her arms wrapped around her knees and was watching the activity on the film set.

"There's Montana," said Charlotte. "Let's go and meet her."

They sat down on the grass next to the girl.

"Hi," she said, pushing her sunglasses on top of her head. "Can you believe we're on the set of *Elf Wars*?"

"It's pretty amazing," agreed Charlotte. "By the way, I'm Charlotte and this is Mia."

"I'm Montana," said the girl.

"Are you an actress?" asked Mia.

"Well, I take drama classes," said Montana. "There was a casting call at my school. They needed children to be extras."

"Being in a movie must be like a dream come true," said Charlotte.

"Yes, but I really wish I could get a speaking part," said Montana longingly.

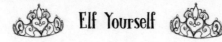

"I want to be a movie star like Grace Devlin when I grow up."

Charlotte caught Mia's eye and winked. Now they knew what Montana had wished for on the tiara star!

"We love Grace Devlin, too," Charlotte told Montana. *Phew*, she thought, *I didn't call her Princess Grace this time.*

The lady with the clapperboard approached the group of children. "I'm Rachel, the director's assistant," she told them. "You all need to get into your costumes now."

Montana scrambled to her feet.

"Do you think we should go with them?" whispered Mia worriedly.

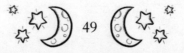

Charlotte nodded. "Hopefully everyone will think that we're extras too," she whispered back.

Charlotte and Mia followed Montana and the other extras into the big wardrobe trailer. An assistant handed Montana a floaty pale green and yellow dress and she ducked behind a screen to get changed.

"You look great," said Charlotte when Montana came out in her costume. The dress looked like it was made from petals.

"I feel like an elf already," Montana said, sticking out her foot to show the girls her green slippers with curled-up toes.

"Everyone please head over to hair and make-up now," said the wardrobe lady.

The girls followed Montana to the next trailer along. Luckily Montana was too excited to question why Mia and Charlotte hadn't put on their own costumes.

Montana sat down in front of a mirror surrounded by light bulbs. A trendy-looking lady with cropped pink hair, denim shorts and a nose ring wheeled a trolley full of make-up over to her.

"Hi, I'm Suzanne," the make-up artist said, snapping her chewing gum. "Is this your first day on set?"

Montana nodded. "It's my only day on set. My parents don't want me missing more than one day of school."

"The movie's going to be a huge hit," said Suzanne, brushing some powder on Montana's face.

"What's it about?" asked Mia.

"It's a fantasy story," explained Suzanne. "It's about an evil troll called Org who's trying to take over a magical kingdom."

"Are there any big stars in the movie?" asked Charlotte.

"Loads! Lachlan Murphy plays the elf

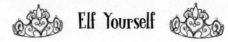
prince," said Suzanne as she dusted powder on Montana's face.

"Oh my goodness!" gasped Charlotte, suddenly remembering the scene they had just watched. "I can't believe that was him!" Lachlan Murphy was the star of the twins' favourite space movies.

"He looks different in his silvery wig," said Suzanne as she painted glittery swirls on Montana's cheeks. "Even though he's really famous, he's a lovely guy."

"Maybe I'll get to meet him," said Montana. "He might help me get a speaking part."

"Ew," said Mia, as Suzanne picked up something floppy. "What are those?"

"Your friend's new elf ears," said Suzanne, grinning.

The make-up artist dipped a brush into special glue and painted it over one of the rubbery ears. She stuck it in place over Montana's right ear, then she did the same on the left side. The fake ears were pointy, like the ones the elf prince had been wearing.

"They look so real!" said Mia.

Charlotte touched one of Montana's pointy ears. "It feels real, too!"

As a finishing touch, Suzanne dabbed some colour on Montana's lips. "Ta da!" she said. "You're camera-ready now!"

The director's assistant stuck her head

round the make-up trailer's door. "Extras are needed on set in five minutes," Rachel said.

Montana frowned at Mia and Charlotte. "Don't you need to get into costume?" she asked them.

"Er …" said Mia.

Before Charlotte could think up an excuse, an actor dressed as an ugly green troll barged into the make-up trailer.

Even though Charlotte knew it was just a costume, the troll sent chills up her spine – he looked truly evil. He seemed to be in character already.

The troll pushed past Montana, sending her crashing into a make-up trolley. "Oi! Out of my way!" he snapped in a strangely familiar voice.

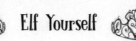

"Montana!" gasped Mia, running over to help her up.

As Montana stood, Charlotte saw that her beautiful costume was covered in blood. It was dripping down her dress and pooling around her curly-toed shoes.

"Oh no!" she cried. "You're hurt!"

"No," said Montana. "I'm fine." She bent to pick up a red bottle that had fallen off the make-up trolley and splashed her. "It's fake blood."

"Wait a minute," said Charlotte, narrowing her eyes at the troll. "I know who that is." Under the green make-up and fake warts she recognised the sneering face of Hex – Princess Poison's horrible helper!

"What am I going to do?" Montana said, staring at her stained dress in dismay. "My costume is ruined!"

"Oh dear," said Hex, smirking nastily. "Montana won't get a speaking part now. She won't get to be in the movie at all!"

CHAPTER FOUR
Extra Extras

"He's right," said Montana, her eyes brimming with tears. "This was my big chance to get noticed, but I might as well go home now." Sobbing, she ran out of the make-up trailer.

"Wait!" cried Charlotte, dashing after Montana.

"We can help you!" said Mia.

Montana turned back to them. "How?" she sniffled.

"Come with us," asked Charlotte, ducking behind one of the movie trailers. Mia and Charlotte held their glowing pendants together, forming a heart.

"I wish for Montana's costume to be fixed," said Mia.

With a flash of golden light the fake blood vanished and Montana's costume was even better than before. But it wasn't her own clothes that Montana was staring at in astonishment …

Charlotte turned to Mia and gasped. Her friend was wearing a filmy pale blue dress with tiny silver sequins that sparkled like dewdrops. Her hair had been curled and topped with a crown of delicate blue flowers. Pointy elf ears poked out from under it.

"You look like an elf," Charlotte told Mia.

"So do you!" replied Mia.

Charlotte glanced down and saw that she was wearing a brown and orange dress that seemed to be made from autumn leaves.

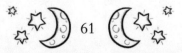

Soft suede boots laced up her legs. She touched her ears. They were pointy!

"We get to be in the movie too!" said Charlotte.

"H-how did you do that?" stammered Montana.

"Last call for extras," Rachel's voice crackled over the sound system.

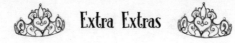

"We'll explain later," said Charlotte. Holding hands, the three girls sprinted back to the film set.

The extras had gathered in a clearing by the woods. Lights and microphones were positioned all around it.

"You'll be dancing in a fairy circle," explained the director. "When the elf prince walks past, you will all bow to him." She did a low, sweeping bow to demonstrate.

The extras practised dancing in a circle. Lachlan Murphy, the movie star playing the elf prince, strode into the clearing. On the director's cue, the extras bowed.

"That looked great," said the director. "I think we're ready to roll. Places, everyone."

She took her position behind the movie camera, which was mounted on a wheeled cart. "And … action!" she called.

CLACK! Rachel snapped the clapperboard shut and the movie camera started filming. As she danced with the other extras, Charlotte watched Montana's beaming face. When the elf prince walked into the clearing, Montana's expression changed to one of awe. *Wow,* thought Charlotte, *she's good.*

"Take two!" called the director, zooming the camera into Montana's face.

CLACK! Rachel snapped the clapperboard shut again and they filmed the scene again. They did it two more times, until finally the director was satisfied.

"Cut!" she called. "Let's take a break. You can all head over to craft services."

"Oooh! I love doing crafts," said Mia.

Lachlan Murphy overheard her and smiled. "Craft services is what we call the cafeteria on a movie set," he explained kindly. "I'll show you where it is."

Mia's cheeks flushed pink underneath her glittery make-up. She was too starstruck to reply to the famous actor.

But Charlotte grinned at Lachlan. "My twin brothers are obsessed with *Space Safari*."

"Ooh! I love that movie too," said Montana. She did a perfect imitation of Lachlan's character in *Space Safari*.

"You're good," Lachlan said, grinning. "I'd better watch out or you'll put me out of a job. Are you hoping to be an actor when you grow up?"

Montana nodded. "How did you get your big break?" she asked the movie star.

"I was working on a film as a cameraman,

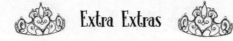

but the director thought I looked right for a part," Lachlan said as they strolled across the set. "I got cast and the rest is history."

"I hope I get a lucky break too," said Montana.

"I think we just have," said Charlotte, her mouth watering as she spied a table heaving with platters of sandwiches, bowls of salad and fruit, trays of hot pasta and freshly baked cakes and cookies.

"So are you enjoying being on a movie set?" asked Lachlan.

Mia nodded shyly.

"It's cool," said Charlotte, serving herself some pasta. "But the story doesn't make any sense. The scene we just filmed doesn't

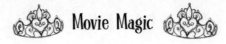

follow on from the one before it."

"Movies aren't filmed in sequence," explained Lachlan. "After all the filming is done, the scenes get edited into the right order."

"Hey, Lachlan," Charlotte said as the actor helped himself to a drink. "What type of bread do elves eat?"

The actor looked puzzled. "I've never really thought about it."

"*Short*bread!" said Charlotte.

The star's face broke into a dazzling smile as he realised it was a joke. "I'll tell that to the rest of the cast," he chuckled. "I'd better go and learn my lines for the next scene," he added, grabbing a sandwich and heading to his private trailer.

As soon as he was out of earshot, Montana blurted out, "How did you do that thing with the costumes? Was it special effects?"

Mia checked whether anyone was listening. "It wasn't special effects," she whispered. "It was magic."

"Magic?" said Montana, confused. "As in movie magic?"

"No," said Mia. "Real magic."

"Mia and I are training to become Secret Princesses," explained Charlotte. "We can use magic to help grant the wish you made on a star."

"But things like that only happen in the movies!" said Montana, her eyes shining with excitement.

"Well, we *are* in a movie," Mia said, smiling. "And we're going to do whatever we can to get you a speaking part in it!"

After eating lunch they went back to the make-up trailer.

"We met Lachlan Murphy," Charlotte

said as Suzanne touched up the powder on her nose. "He was really nice."

"His co-star is lovely too," said Suzanne. "She's—"

"Extras, report to Location Three," Rachel's voice cut in over the sound system.

The extras followed signs to Location Three – a babbling brook with a waterfall in the background. Nearby, lights shone down on a magnificent white Pegasus standing on a rock at the edge of the stream.

"This is an important scene," the director explained. "The elf prince asks the Pegasus to take a message to the fairy queen."

"Everyone must be really careful around the Pegasus," Rachel warned the extras.

"It's a very important piece of equipment." She pressed some buttons on a remote control and the Pegasus spread its wings.

"Ooh!" gasped the children.

Rachel pressed a different button and the Pegasus lowered his head and stamped one of his hooves.

"It took over a year to build," said the director proudly, "and cost over a million."

"It looks exactly like Snowdrop!" Mia whispered to Charlotte.

The mention of Snowdrop reminded Charlotte of their friends at Wishing Star Palace. "We've got to grant Montana's wish," she whispered. "Princess Luna's counting on us."

"We'll need to be on our guard," Mia whispered back. "Hex almost got Montana kicked off the movie, so we know Princess Poison is trying to spoil her wish."

"Take your places, everyone!" called Rachel.

The extras knelt down by the brook.

"Action!" called the director.

The elf prince respectfully approached the Pegasus. He gently placed his hand on the creature's nose and began to say his line. "Oh, mighty Pega—"

"Cut!" cried the director. She frowned as she watched the scene again on the monitor. "I'm picking up two weird blue lights," she said. "Move the Pegasus to the

rehearsal area while we investigate," she added, signalling to her assistants.

Looking down at her hand, Charlotte suddenly realised where the light was coming from. Her sapphire ring was flashing – and so was Mia's. Danger was nearby!

CHAPTER FIVE
Snowdrop to the Rescue!

"Look at that cute little robot," said
Montana. "What scene do you think
it's in?"

Mia and Charlotte craned their necks
to see what Montana was looking at.
Charlotte's heart sank when she recognised
the small white robot with the bright green
flashing eyes.

"Oh no," she groaned. It was EVA, Princess Poison's Extra Villainous Assistant. Princess Poison had cursed the robot so that it obeyed her evil commands.

"So that's why our rings are flashing," muttered Mia as the robot wheeled towards them.

"What's it holding?" asked Montana.

The robot had a remote control in its hand. EVA jabbed several buttons and the

Pegasus started to flap its wings wildly. The robot pressed more buttons and the Pegasus stamped its hooves.

The director and the film crew were huddled around the monitors, unaware of what was going on.

"Stop that!" hissed Mia.

"USER NOT RECOGNISED," said EVA.

"COMMAND FAILED."

EVA poked more buttons on the remote control. Now the Pegasus stamped its hooves, nodded its head, flapped its wings and swished its tail – all at the same time!

Charlotte darted forward and tried to wrestle the remote control out of the robot's hand. "Give me that!"

The remote control flew out of EVA's hand and landed on the ground by Montana.

CRUNCH!

EVA's wheels rolled over the remote control, crushing it.

The Pegasus's movements became jerky as it flew towards the brook. Smoke poured out of the winged horse.

"What's wrong?" the director shouted, suddenly noticing the smoke.

"The circuits must have overloaded," said one of the crew.

With one final judder, the Pegasus keeled over and fell into the stream.

SPLASH!

"No!" screamed the director as the winged horse lay in the water.

Rachel picked up the crushed remote control. She glared at Montana. "What have you done?"

"I didn't touch it," protested Montana. "It was the robot!"

They turned around but EVA was gone.

79

"The only robot here was the Pegasus,"
Rachel said. "And thanks to you it's
ruined."

"You're fired!" the director shouted at
Montana. "I'll make sure you never work on
a movie again!"

Montana gulped, her bottom lip
trembling.

"We've got to do something!" Charlotte
said. She held her pendant against Mia's.

"I wish for a Pegasus," said Mia.

There was a flash of light and a splashing
noise. A gorgeous white Pegasus climbed
out of the stream. It shook itself dry, then
trotted over to Mia and nuzzled her in a
friendly way. All around, the film crew were

carrying on as if they hadn't noticed the
magical change.

"That's Snowdrop!" gasped Mia.

"Yes," agreed Charlotte. "It looks just
like him."

"No," said Mia. "It really is Snowdrop!"

The winged horse whickered softly and
nodded his head.

Charlotte stroked Snowdrop's silky mane. "Thanks for helping us," she whispered.

Snowdrop trotted over to the rocks.

"OK, we're ready to film," said the director, sitting down behind her camera.

"Take two!" said Rachel, snapping her clapperboard shut.

As the cameras rolled, the elf prince approached Snowdrop. "Oh, mighty Pegasus," Lachlan said, "the creatures of the magic realm need your help."

Snowdrop whinnied and pawed the ground with his hoof.

Lachlan placed his hand on Snowdrop's velvety nose. "Will you carry a message to the Fairy Queen for me?" he pleaded.

"Tell her that if the elves and fairies work together we can defeat the troll army."

Snowdrop tossed his head, his silky white mane falling over his gorgeous grey eyes. Then the Pegasus reared up, his hooves pawing the air. Dropping back down to the ground, Snowdrop galloped away from the elf prince. He beat his wings and soared up into the sky.

"Godspeed!" cried Lachlan. "Return to us soon!"

"Cut!" called the director. "That was perfect!"

"The Pegasus is brilliant," said Lachlan. "It's hard to believe it's a robot."

Because it isn't! thought Charlotte,

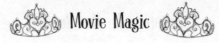

sharing a secret smile with Mia.

As the crew got ready for the next scene, Montana hurried over to the girls. "Did you do magic again?" she asked them breathlessly.

Mia nodded. "We couldn't let you get the blame for something you didn't do."

"Why isn't everyone freaked out?" Montana asked. "I mean one minute the director fired me, the next it was like nothing had gone wrong."

Charlotte shrugged. "That's just how the magic works."

"Can you make another wish right now?" asked Montana eagerly. "So that I get a speaking part?"

"Our magic isn't powerful enough to do that," said Mia. "We can only make three small wishes to help you out."

As Montana headed over to the food table to get a drink, Charlotte turned to Mia. "How are we going to get Montana a speaking part?"

"I have no idea," said Mia, frowning. "We've managed to stop Hex and EVA from getting Montana fired – but that hasn't helped get her a bigger part."

Charlotte sighed. "We just have to hope that if she's in a few more scenes she'll get noticed – the way Lachlan did."

Montana returned with water for all of them, and they headed to the next location.

An enormous green screen had been rigged up, blocking out all the movie trailers and equipment behind it. Assistants handed extras baskets that looked like acorns.

"This next scene is set at the fairy market," explained the director.

The girls exchanged puzzled looks.

Charlotte raised her hand. "Excuse me," she said. "But where's the market?"

The director chuckled. "Sorry, I forgot that you haven't been on a movie set before," she said. "The fairy market will be added in later using computer animation."

"We shoot against a green screen because it makes it easier to add in the background," added Rachel.

A harsh voice behind the girls hissed, "And green just happens to be my favourite colour."

Charlotte spun around and saw a tall woman in a green dress and spiky high heels. She had jet-black hair with a white-blonde steak in it and her green eyes glinted maliciously.

"Go away, Princess Poison," said Charlotte. "This movie has a baddie already."

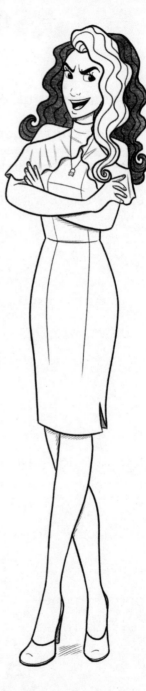

"You're right," sneered Princess Poison. "Not everyone gets to be a movie star. Just like not every tiara star wish gets granted!"

CHAPTER SIX
The Fairy Market

"We've already granted three of the tiara star wishes," said Charlotte defiantly. "And we'll grant the last one too. Montana will have a part in the movie!"

"We'll see about that," said Princess Poison smugly, pulling out her wand.

She pointed it at the green screen and hissed a spell:

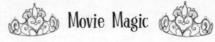

Wishing on a tiara star was a big mistake.
Now Montana won't get her lucky break!

There was a flash of green light and
suddenly the blue sky turned grey. The trees
in the woods swayed as strong gusts of wind
shook their branches and leaves.

WHOOSH!

A violent gale ripped the green screen
from its supports. It flew into the air and
blew away, billowing over the woods like an
enormous green parachute.

"What a shame," said Princess Poison.
"The weather seems to have turned."

"Everyone back to the trailers. Filming
suspended until tomorrow," the director

shouted through a megaphone.

"Toodles!" cried Princess Poison, waving her wand and vanishing.

Extras ran to take shelter as hailstones pelted down. But Montana stood rooted to the spot, staring at the sky in dismay. "I'm only an extra for today," she said sadly.

"My parents won't let me miss another day of school!"

"Don't worry," Charlotte shouted over the howling wind. "We can fix this!"

She and Mia held their pendants together as hailstones pinged off their backs. The half-hearts were glowing very faintly, because there was only enough magic to make one more wish.

"I wish for the fairy market scene to go ahead," said Mia.

There was a flash of light and the skies cleared. The wind dropped to a gentle breeze and the sun came out again. But now, instead of a big green screen, there was a fairy market in the clearing!

Wooden stalls with giant red and white toadstools for tables displayed beautiful fairy goods for sale. There were lacy dresses made out of cobwebs, shiny bangles and dainty cups made from fairy gold, and magical potions and lotions in colourful glass bottles. It looked exactly how Charlotte imagined a fairy market should be, except for the lights, microphones and movie cameras dotted around it.

"Places please, everyone," called the director. "We're ready to shoot."

The actors and extras playing fairies and elves returned to the set and took their places. Rachel snapped her clapperboard and filming began.

Mia and Charlotte linked arms with
Montana, chatting as they strolled through
the fairy market.

"This is amazing!" breathed Montana,
gazing around with eyes as big as saucers.

"Try before you buy," said an actress
playing a fairy, waving them over. She
offered them a plate of tiny fairy cakes

covered in sugared violets and rose petals.

"Mmm," said Charlotte, biting into a cake.

"Get your lucky charms here!" called an actor dressed as an elf. His stall was covered in all sorts of trinkets and crystals.

A camera panned past the girls as they examined the elf's wares.

"Do you think these work?" asked Montana, holding up a necklace with a good-luck charm. "Maybe if I had one I'd get a speaking part."

"It's just a movie prop," said Mia. "Besides, you don't need luck – you've got talent."

Charlotte nodded. "Even Lachlan Murphy thought so, remember."

"Charms to ward off the evil!" called the elf, holding up a blue glass ornament shaped like an eye.

"Now that would be handy," said Charlotte.

"Who was that mean lady who changed the weather?" asked Montana as they moved on. "She can do magic like you."

"Not like us," said Mia, shaking her head. "She does BAD magic."

"Her name is Princess Poison," said Charlotte. "She's trying to spoil your wish. The robot and the troll who bumped into you both work for her."

"I hope she doesn't come back to the film set," said Montana.

"Me too," said Mia. "We used up our last wish, so now we don't have any magic left to stop her."

"But don't worry," Charlotte said quickly, noticing Montana's worried expression. "We've never let her stop us from granting a wish and we're not about to start now."

"Cut!" shouted the director, clapping her hands. "Great work, everyone. We've got one more scene to film today – the epic battle between the troll army and the fairy folk."

"The script says there's a big explosion at the end of the battle," said someone in a fairy costume, sounding nervous.

"That's right," said the director. She

pointed to some boxes marked *Danger –
Fireworks*. "The Fairy Queen uses her magic
to blow up Org's cave. But don't worry.
We'll be using specially trained stuntmen
for that scene."

A props assistant gave the elves and
fairies swords to use. They looked very
real, but the blades weren't sharp. "Time to
rehearse the battle scene!" he called.

"I challenge you to a duel!" said
Charlotte, swishing her fake sword high in
the air.

Giggling, Mia pretended that Charlotte
was a troll.

"Take that, you naughty troll!" she said,
clashing swords with her best friend.

"Charlotte! Mia!" yelled Montana. "She's back!

Charlotte spun round and saw Princess Poison stalking towards them. Hex, still in his troll costume, was trailing behind her.

"You're all having far too much fun," said Princess Poison, glowering at Mia and Charlotte. "Well, the fun ends now!"

She turned to her assistant. "I don't know about you, Hex, but I think this scene needs to start with a BANG." She pointed her wand at the boxes of fireworks.

"No!" gasped Mia. "You can't set those off – people could get hurt!"

"Don't be silly," said Princess Poison. "Everyone loves a good fireworks display."

Charlotte ran forward to snatch Princess Poison's wand but Hex held her back.

Princess Poison started to growl a spell:

> **It's time for you little brats
> to hit the road,
> So I'm going to make these
> fireworks exp–**

"Elves! Fairies!" interupted Montana, holding her sword high in the air like a warrior. "Prepare to fight!"

The extras cheered and waved their swords in the air.

Princess Poison broke off from her spell and put her hands on her hips, glaring at Montana in annoyance.

"Attack!" commanded Montana.

Every elf and fairy on the movie set charged forward, waving their swords.

"Let go of her!" shouted an elf, pointing his sword at Hex.

"Yikes!" shrieked Hex, dropping Charlotte's arms. He ran away as fast as his short legs would carry him.

Charlotte quickly joined in with the fight. She charged forward, her sword swiping at Princess Poison's wand. *SWISH!*

Princess Poison fought back, jabbing her wand in all directions to fend off her attackers.

Mia lunged forward, swinging her sword just like the stuntman had showed them. *SWASH!*

"Surrender!" demanded Mia and Charlotte, pointing their swords at Princess Poison.

Princess Posion's eyes darted around, looking for an escape. But it was no use. The elves and fairies had her completely surrounded.

 **Movie Magic**

"Aaargghh!" shrieked Princess Poison
in frustration. She waved her wand and
vanished in a flash of green light.

CHAPTER SEVEN
Drama Queen

"Yay!" cheered the elf and fairy extras. "We beat the baddies!"

Mia and Charlotte hugged Montana. "Thank you so much," said Charlotte. "You got rid of Princess Poison."

"Well, I wasn't going to let her hurt my friends," said Montana.

"That's what Princess Poison never

remembers," said Mia. "That friendship is
more powerful than magic."

"What a terrific rehearsal!" the director
told the extras. "You can all take a short
break. Except for you," she added, pointing
at Montana.

"Me?" said Montana, surprised.

"I watched you rehearse," the director
said. "It was great how you rallied the
troops."

"Thanks," said Montana, glowing with
pride.

"In fact, I think we should put a line like
that in the movie – would you like to say it?
It would mean you have a speaking role,"
said the director.

Montana stared
at the director,
speechless.

"She says yes,"
piped up Charlotte,
nudging Montana.

"Yes!" squealed
Montana.

"Great," said the director.
"Then there's someone you should meet.
She's just coming now."

"Oh my gosh," gasped Montana, staring
across the movie set.

Charlotte turned to look. A tall actress
was approaching them. She was wearing
a regal white gown with gauzy wings.

A silver crown perched on her long, blonde hair and she was carrying a silver sword and shield. But despite the blonde wig and the fact that she wasn't wearing her glasses, Charlotte recognised her instantly. "It's—"

"Princess Grace," Mia whispered.

"She's playing the Fairy Queen," said Charlotte.

"Places for the battle scene, please!" the director called.

The army of elves and fairies stood behind the Fairy Queen and the Elf Prince on the crest of a small hill. The sun was beginning to set in the distance, painting the sky above the woods with streaks of pink and purple. Movie cameras were positioned all around the battlefield.

"And … action!" called the director as Rachel snapped her clapperboard.

"Your Highness," shouted Montana, pointing to the bottom of the hill. "The troll army is on the march!"

Princess Grace turned to the extras, holding her arms out wide to her subjects.

"Together we will defeat evil," she said in a calm, clear voice. "We will never give up our kingdom!"

"Charge!" cried Montana.

The elves and fairies surged down the hill, attacking the trolls.

"Cut!" cried the director. "We got it in one take. That's a wrap for today!"

"Did you see that?" asked Montana, running over to Mia and Charlotte. "I got a speaking part!"

"You were brilliant," said Mia. "I'm sure you'll be a big star one day."

"I can't believe that I'm in a movie with Grace Devlin," Montana said, beaming. "Thanks so much for helping me."

Suddenly, all of the actors playing fairies rose into the air, their wings fluttering as they swooped and soared high above the movie set.

"The special effects on this movie are incredible," said Lachlan in amazement, glancing up at the sky on his way back to his trailer.

Princess Grace winked at Mia and Charlotte. They knew it wasn't special effects – it was magic, because they had granted Montana's wish!

"We've got to go now," Charlotte told Montana.

"We'll go and see the movie when it comes out," Mia promised.

"I'll always think of you two when I look up at the stars," said Montana. "I'll never forget what you did for me." Waving goodbye, she headed off to the wardrobe trailer.

"Look, Mia!" said Charlotte. EVA was back! The little robot was wheeling around and around the set in circles, its green eyes flashing in the dusk.

"ERROR 103. USER NOT RECOGNISED," the robot repeated over and over, sounding forlorn.

"What a cute robot," said the director. "I can use this little guy in my next movie." She scooped up the robot and walked off.

Charlotte grinned at Mia. "Looks like Montana isn't the only one getting a lucky break today."

Princess Grace came over to the girls, smiling. "Let's go to my trailer."

The girls followed Grace into her big, silver trailer.

"I would have invited you in earlier," said Grace. "But I was busy doing interviews in here all day."

"This is so posh!" exclaimed Charlotte, looking around. There was a sitting area with leather sofas, an enormous television and a table set out with snacks. "I feel like a star!"

"You are a star!" Grace said, "Both of you girls are. You granted the last tiara star wish. Now it's time for you to go back to the palace to celebrate." She opened the door of her trailer and whistled.

A winged horse trotted over, tossing his silky mane.

"Snowdrop," said Princess Grace, "take the girls back to the palace, please."

Mia and Charlotte climbed on to Snowdrop's back.

Charlotte gripped his mane, feeling
Mia's arms tighten around her waist as the
Pegasus beat his wings and rose into the
air. She looked down and saw the movie set
getting smaller and smaller far below them.

"Whee!" Charlotte cried as they soared
through the stars. The Tiara Constellation's
stars sparkled like diamonds, the four stars

at the tips lighting up the dark.

All too soon, the ride was over. Snowdrop set them down in the middle of the glamping ground. Princess Luna ran down the steps of the treehouse to greet them.

"You did it!" she cried, hugging them both. "Let's see if my magic's back!" She touched her wand to Mia's pendant and a fourth white moonstone appeared in the necklace. Then she tapped Charlotte's necklace and a milky white gem appeared in her pendant, too.

Luna waved her wand and the moonstones in their pendants suddenly vanished. Now, on their wrists, Mia and Charlotte wore beautiful moonstone bracelets!

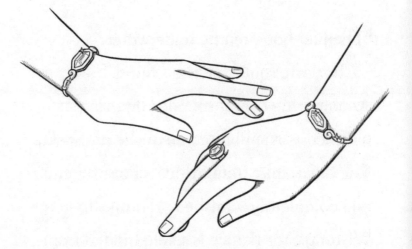

The other princesses came out of their
tents and caravans to congratulate the girls.

"You're ready to start on the next stage of
your training!" Alice said.

"What's that?" asked Mia.

"You'll need to grant four wishes to earn
your aquamarine comb," said Princess
Sylvie. She plucked a silver comb with
blue gems out of her red hair to show them.

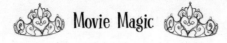 Movie Magic

"They let you breathe underwater."

Charlotte squeezed Mia's hand. Aquamarine combs sounded amazing!

Princess Evie pointed up at the night sky. The green mist from Princess Poison's curse had completely vanished. "Thanks to you, Wishing Star Palace is safely hidden from view," she said.

"Hurrah!" cheered all of the Secret Princesses.

"Oh, it's so good to have my magic back," said Princess Luna. "I want to do some more magic to celebrate."

She pointed her wand at the sky.

BANG! A firework shaped like a flower burst into the air. Pink and purple sparkles rained down above the palace.

"Oooh!" gasped the Secret Princesses.

BOOM! Another firework went off, sending glittering trails of red and white swirling in the dark sky.

Charlotte and Mia held hands and watched the beautiful firework display.

 **Movie Magic**

The grand finale went on for ages, as colourful rockets, fountains and Catherine wheels danced across the night sky.

When it was over, Princess Luna smiled at the girls. "It's time for you to go home now," she told them.

"See you soon, Mia," Charlotte said, hugging her best friend goodbye.

"To start earning aquamarines," whispered Mia, hugging her back.

Princess Luna waved her wand and the magic swept the girls away from the palace.

A moment later, Charlotte was back home in her bathroom. She grinned at her reflection in the mirror. She was one step closer to becoming a Secret Princess.

Her half-heart pendant might be empty now – but Charlotte knew that soon it would be filled with beautiful aquamarines. And best of all, she'd be earning them with her friend Mia!

The End

Join Charlotte and Mia in their
next Secret Princesses adventure

Bridemaid
Surprise

Read on for a sneak peek!

Bridemaid Surprise

"Can I have cheese on my burger, please?" asked Mia Thompson. Her mouth watered as the delicious smell wafted from the barbecue.

"One cheeseburger, coming right up," said Mia's dad, flipping a burger on the grill.

"I want a sausage!" cried Mia's little sister, Elsie.

Mia and Elsie were spending the weekend at their dad's flat. Most of the time they lived with their mum, but every other weekend they visited their dad. It had been hard to get used to at first, but now Mia and Elsie looked forward to their weekends with Dad – he always planned fun things to do with them.

"Come on, Elsie," said Mia. "Let's go inside and set the table."

The girls crossed the tiny garden and went into the kitchen through the patio doors. Opening a cupboard, Mia took out plates and drinking glasses while Elsie rummaged in the cutlery drawer for knives and forks.

Mia opened the fridge, which was covered in photos of the girls and pictures that they had drawn. She took out a bowl of salad and a bottle of lemonade.

"Ooh!" said Elsie excitedly. "Mum never buys fizzy drinks."

Mia and Elsie grinned at each other. There were definitely advantages to having two different homes!

Read Bridemaid
Surprise to find out
what happens next!

Acting Advice

Do you want to be an actor like Montana?
Here are some acting tips to help you become a
star of the stage and screen!

1. Really understand your character. What kind of person are they? What are their likes and dislikes?

2. Act using your whole body, not just your voice. How does your character walk? What kind of gestures do they use?

3. Breathe deeply and project your voice so everyone in the audience can hear you

4. Learn your lines well. If you forget one, don't apologise – just keep going

5. When another actor is talking, really listen to them

6. If you get stage fright, try acting in front of a small audience first until you build up confidence

7. Listen to feedback so you can get better. In a movie or play, the director gives the actors tips for how to improve their performance

8. Learn from great actors. Watch movies and go to the theatre as much as you can. Think about what made an actor's performance good or bad

Secret
PRINCESSES

What would you wish for?

Are you a Secret Princess?

Join the Secret Princesses Club at:

secretprincessesbooks.co.uk

Explore the magic of the
Secret Princesses and discover:

♥ Special competitions! ♥
♥ Exclusive content! ♥
♥ All the latest princess news! ♥